Wing Nuts: Screwy Haiku

by Paul B. Janeczko and J. Patrick Lewis

illustrated by Tricia Tusa

LITTLE, BROWN AND COMPANY
New York ⋅ Boston

Little, Brown and Company

Time Warner Book Group • 1271 Avenue of the Americas, New York, NY 10020
Visit our Web site at www.lb-kids.com

First Edition: April 2006

Library of Congress Cataloging-in-Publication Data

Lewis, J. Patrick.
  Wing nuts : screwy haiku / by J. Patrick Lewis and Paul B. Janeczko :
illustrated by Tricia Tusa.— 1st ed.
    p. cm.
  ISBN 0-316-60731-2
  1. Children's poetry, American. 2. Senryu, American. I. Janeczko, Paul B.
II. Tusa, Tricia, ill. III. Title.
PS3562.E9465W56 2006
811'.54 — dc22

2005007970

10 9 8 7 6 5 4 3 2 1

Book design by Saho Fujii

SC

Printed in China

The illustrations for this book were done in
ink and watercolor on Fabriano 140# paper.
The text was set in Birdlegs
and the display type is Bodoni Sev Swash and Ojaio.

For Emma and the Posse
—P.B.J.

For Kelly and Scott Marceau
—J.P.L.

For Vivian
—T.T.

Insect photographer
introduces himself:

I'm a shutterbug

Hippo and baby
giant tater and tot
hippo-*potato*-mus

Solitary crow
calls its cousin in distant pine
with its

cawing card

High school band minus
its tuba player—looking
for a substi-*toot!*

Swift punishment
for drinking from milk carton ...
mouthful of curdles

Irksome mosquito,
kindly sing your evening song

Mice dart in shadows
as barn cat waits and grins . . .
Ah! fast food tonight

Grumpy bear growl
blends with chirp of rusty hinge . . .
Mom and Dad snoring

My older sister
gets a complete makeover—
very mascary!

Freedom vanishes
as the babysitter arrives ...
kids are tied in *nots*

Tabby and Fido
do whatever they want—
reigning cat and dog

Yellowstone campsite picnickers hoping dinner is un-*bear*-able

Noah Webster had
no choice except to put
the cart before the horse

Traveling circus—
the knife thrower
hiccups

Sluggish squirrel lurches across the busy highway to the other si—

Kid eyes the coins
left on the sunny dashboard . . .
Off with hot money!

On Ferris wheel
I regret French fries, milk shake—
those below agree

Jumping double dutch
over the L.A. summer—
the Queen of the Hop

Lions versus gazelles!
game of speed of game—
zebra referees

Grandpa's underwear
pulled up so high—
a chest of drawers

City pigeons chatter
and coo—busybodies
eavesdropping

O warm summer night
I awake to rude music:
cat coughing up hair ball

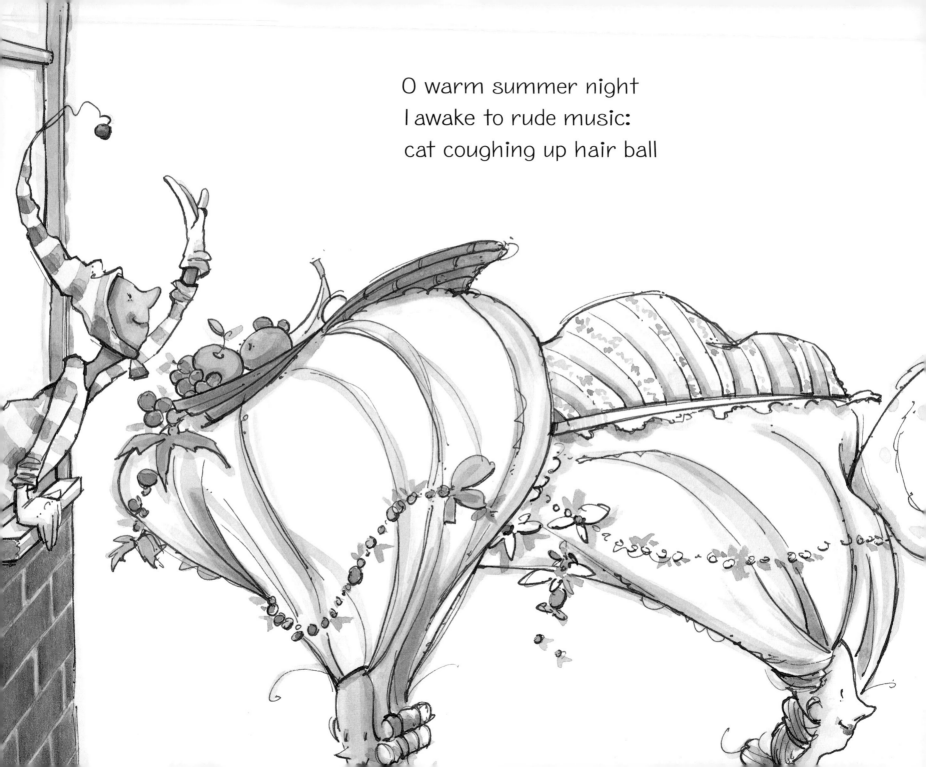

A senryu goes
bouncing along into . . .

a giant poet-tree!